Earl's Big Adventure in Japan

Written by Hanna Haidar
Illustrated by Kimberly Newton

It was a cold winter day and Earl was stretched out by the fire warming his little monkey toes. He was reading a book when he heard the doorbell and saw his good friend John standing by the window. Earl let John into the house and saw that he was VERY excited.

John reached into his pocket and pulled out a small brown envelope.

"Can you guess what's inside?" he asked.

They had been friends for a long time so Earl had a good guess.

"Plane tickets?" He hoped he was right.

"That's right Earl…it's time for us to have another adventure!"

Earl ran for a map of the world. Where on earth could they be going? John pointed to a chain of islands in the Pacific Ocean.

"How would you like to go snowboarding in Japan?" Earl was so excited, he almost fell over!

After lots of planning and packing, they left their homes on Cape Cod and began the long trip from Boston to Tokyo where Earl got a new stamp in his passport.

From Tokyo they flew to the city of Sapporo on Japan's northern island of Hokkaido. From Sapporo they took a train up into the mountains to a resort named Niseko. Earl couldn't wait to get there! Monkeys are VERY fidgety on planes and trains so to pass the time they practiced learning new words in Japanese.

The train ride was beautiful and Earl and John were very excited because it snowed the whole way there.

The next morning Earl and John woke up to a white blanket of fresh powdery snow. They put on their snowboarding gear and walked to the mountain. Earl looked up at the mountain and felt a little scared…it was HUGE!

John saw that Earl was nervous and said "Earl, don't worry, we don't have to start at the top. We'll start on the easy trails and when you feel comfortable, we can do harder ones."

Earl felt better; he was worried John was going to want to go to the top!

Earl loved sliding sideways down the mountain on his snowboard. "Woooohoooo" he yelled as he looked back and saw all the snow spraying from his board. "Can we go higher up?" he asked John.

"Of course we can!"

On the next run they went higher up the mountain and rode past beautiful birch trees. Earl liked how tangled up the snow covered trees looked. He was thinking about how much fun they would be to climb and the next thing he knew, he was tumbling!

"Are you ok, Earl?" John asked. Earl looked like a little blue snowman.

"I'm fine." Earl was laughing hard. He thought it was a very funny tumble! Earl wiped all the snow off his chilly monkey face and they rode together down to the bottom where Earl had a big cup of hot chocolate to warm up.

The day flew by and they had lots of fun exploring the mountain. When it was time to stop for dinner, Earl was a little nervous. What would he eat in Japan? They ordered noodles and soon big steaming bowls called ramen were brought out to them.

Earl and John laughed. The bowls were huge!

Earl had fun trying to eat with chopsticks. It took a little practice (and he made a little mess) but he got the hang of it quickly. Soon he was better than John…and the soup was delicious!

The next morning they went back to the mountain and it was busy. Earl saw some children playing in the snow and decided to try out his Japanese. "Ohayou," he said, hoping it meant "good morning."

"Ohayou!" the kids all answered.

Earl had practiced saying "konnichiwa Earl desu" which means "hi my name is Earl."

He hoped it came out right. The kids all understood and soon Earl was making new friends. Some of the kids were learning English in school and they were happy to practice with Earl and help him with his Japanese. Kazu was from Sapporo, Chiyo was from Yokohama, and Yuki was from Tokyo. They worked together to build a giant snowman and it was taller than they were!

Earl and John spent three days snowboarding and playing in the snow. When it was time to leave, Earl felt a little sad to say goodbye to his new friends.

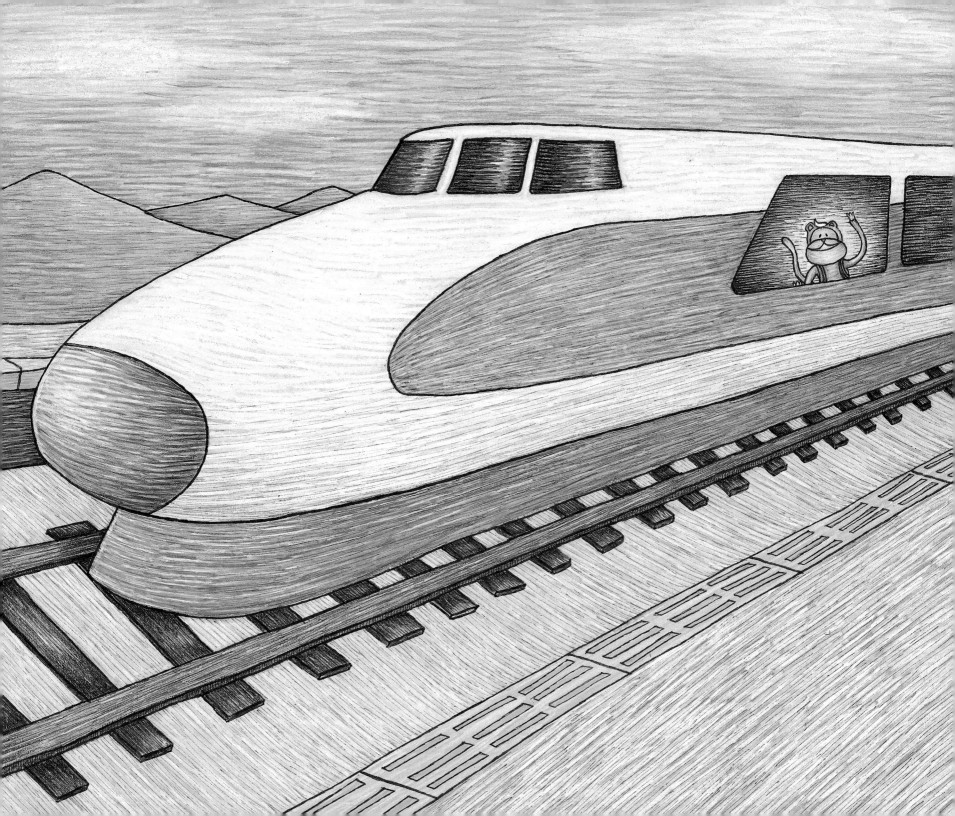

"Don't worry Earl, you are going to love what comes next!" John said.

After a short plane ride to the city of Nagoya, they walked to a train station.

"Another train?" Earl was tired and a little cranky. "What's the big deal?" he thought. John smiled, he knew what Earl was thinking.

"This is a special train. It's called a Shinkansen or bullet train. It goes 186 miles per hour!"

Earl loved riding on the Shinkansen! He stared out the window the whole ride. He sat watching the beautiful Japanese countryside fly by in a blur.

Earl and John arrived in Kyoto to see the famous cherry blossoms which only bloom for a few weeks a year. They walked past ancient temples, modern neon signs, and everywhere their paths were lined by the pretty white and pink cherry trees.

When dinner time came, John asked, "Earl are you feeling brave?"

"Of course!" Earl said and the next thing he knew, John had lead him into a small restaurant. The owners bowed to them and said "irasshaimase!" which means "welcome."

John was happy to hear Earl thank them by saying "arigatou." They had to take off their shoes and they sat around a small table on the floor.

John ordered and soon dinner was in front of them. Earl recognized the little rolls in front of him. "SUSHI???" he yelped. Monkeys don't usually eat raw fish!

"Earl, it's ok. You can have some without fish but you might want to give it a try. It's delicious!"

At first Earl decided to stick with vegetables. He liked the little rolls of rice, cucumber, and carrots. Finally he gathered up all of his monkey courage and tried a piece of sushi with fresh tuna in it. He closed his eyes and took a teeny tiny little bite and he was surprised. It was delicious!

He took the rest of the roll and ate it with one big chomp.

John smiled as Earl tried more types of sushi. He tried salmon, shrimp and some that he couldn't even recognize! The restaurant owner asked Earl if he liked the sushi and Earl answered "oishii!"

Earl could tell John didn't understand the word. "Oishii means it's delicious," Earl explained as he reached for the last piece of sushi.

"I'm very proud of you," John said. "Were you surprised at the taste?"

"Yes," Earl said, "but can we please have ramen tomorrow?" He didn't want to eat fish every day!

After a few days exploring Kyoto, they took another Shinkansen to Tokyo. Earl couldn't believe the lights and crowds. They went to a big square in the city named Shibuya Crossing and watched as hundreds of people crossed the street at the same time. Earl thought it looked fun but very crowded!

When it was time for them to go across, Earl became a little frightened. He was a very small monkey. What if he got run over?
"John, I don't want to go!"

John had a suggestion. "How about a ride on my shoulders?" and Earl thought that sounded fun.

He climbed up and got comfortable. When the light turned green, they stepped into the crosswalk right into the crowd of people coming the other way! Earl looked around and loved the sea of people and all of the big neon lights on the buildings, but he was very happy to be safe up high on John's shoulders!

They spent their final day in Japan walking around Tokyo and enjoyed one last bowl of noodles. Earl was an expert with his chopsticks by now.

John and Earl flew home to Cape Cod and soon Earl was back in front of his fireplace. Earl was feeling a little down that the trip was over so soon; a week had gone by so fast!

"What was your favorite part of the trip?" John asked.

Earl had to think about it. "Playing in the snow with my friends in Niseko."

As John packed up his bag, he gave Earl a big hug. "We've been surfing in Costa Rica and snowboarding in Japan. What do you think we should do next? I'm going to let you decide on the next adventure."

Earl was surprised! There are so many countries to see. How would he choose? Earl spent a long time thinking in front of the fire. Where in the world should they go next?

"My first trip to Japan was just three weeks after the March 2011 earthquake and tsunami. We were amazed at the warm welcome we received everywhere we went. I would like to thank everyone who helped us along our way and showed us so much hospitality during such a challenging time." - Hanna

From flip-flops to snowboard boots, Hanna Haidar loves exploring the outdoors. He also enjoys overseas travel, surfing, motorcycles, cooking, languages and, of course, writing. Many years of international travel inspired the idea of a children's travel series. He has spent the past five winters playing in the snow and working as a snowboard instructor. This is his second book.

Kimberly Newton is a graduate of Massachusetts College of Art & Design who lives in the Boston area. Besides drawing, she's happy to spend the day at the beach, cooking up a storm in the kitchen or hiking through the woods.